BUTTONS

Philip was profoundly deaf and had never uttered a sound. But that was before Buttons, the puppy, came for Christmas and became his best friend. One day, whilst everyone was enjoying a picnic, Buttons went exploring and later, no matter how hard they searched, nobody could find him. Sadly, father reported Buttons' loss to the police. Philip had lost the best friend he had ever known.

In the meantime, Buttons found his way to an Animal Welfare Centre where he made a new friend, Tony. Soon, Buttons was being taught all kinds of skills — he was being trained as a Hearing Dog for the Deaf. Eventually, he was given a new collar and lead and was taken away to a new home. For two hours, Buttons sat patiently in the car, feeling sad that he always lost his best friends; first Philip, and now Tony.

But then the car drew up outside a house, a house that Buttons knew well. And there to greet him was the most marvellous surprise....

A moving story for younger readers. This is Linda Yeatman's first book for Hippo. The charming illustrations are by Sir Hugh Casson.

Buttons

The Dog Who was More than
a Friend

Linda Yeatman

Illustrated by Hugh Casson

Hippo Books
Scholastic Publications Limited
London

Scholastic Publications Ltd.,
10 Earlham Street, London WC2H 9RX, UK

Scholastic Inc.,
730 Broadway, New York, NY 10003, USA

Scholastic Tab Publications Ltd.,
123 Newkirk Road, Richmond Hill,
Ontario L4C 3G5, Canada

Ashton Scholastic Pty. Ltd.,
P O Box 579, Gosford, New South Wales,
Australia

Ashton Scholastic Ltd.,
165 Marua Road, Panmure, Auckland 6,
New Zealand

First published by Piccadilly Press, London 1985

Published in paperback by Scholastic Publications Ltd., 1986

Reprinted 1987

ISBN 0 590 70562 8

Made and printed by Cox and Wyman Ltd., Reading, Berks.
Typeset in Baskerville by CH Print Services, Bromley, Kent.

Introduction

Have you ever wondered what it would be like to live in a silent world? To be surrounded by quiet? No screaming children or barking dogs. No traffic noise or too loud music. Thousands of people DO live in a silent world and for them it is difficult. Deafness is unseen, and because it is unseen it is misunderstood. Many people do not understand that in its own way deafness is a serious disability. Think about it for a minute. Think about not knowing that someone is knocking at your door. Think about not knowing that your mother is calling you. Think about not being able ever to do more than lip-read one person's conversation at a time; about how difficult it would be to talk or play with friends.

That is why Hearing Dogs for the Deaf was created. Hearing Dogs for the Deaf rescues unwanted dogs that have the temperament and intelligence to become good companions. Hearing Dogs for the Deaf trains these dogs to live with profoundly deaf people and to act as ears for them and to tell them that the doorbell is ringing, or the alarm has gone off, or that the baby is crying. If you would like to learn about how you can help sponsor a dog to be named Buttons, please turn to page 53 of this book.

Bruce Fogle DVM MRCVS
Vice Chairman
Hearing Dogs for the Deaf

Chapter One

A Christmas Present

Can you imagine what it would be like to be put in a box and given away as a present on Christmas Day? This is exactly what happened to the dog in this story.

He was born on a farm. At first he lived with his brothers and sisters in a basket under the kitchen table. But when the puppies started to run around, the farmer's wife said, "Enough! Out! These puppies are going to trip me up. They must go out to the barn where they won't be under my feet."

So for the next two or three weeks the puppies romped and chased each other round the barn, and slept on some straw and a blanket in the corner.

Their mother was a beautiful collie who helped with the sheep on the farm. The puppies weren't quite sure who their father was, but they overheard the farmer say they were "proper mongrels" and they felt this was a very fine thing to be. In fact their father was a terrier, so some of the puppies had long silky coats like their mother, and some were wiry and looked more like their father. They were a mixed bunch.

Then, one chilly day, when they were about eight weeks old, one little puppy found himself being lifted up and placed in a cardboard box.

"Help! Help!" he whimpered, as he scrabbled at the sides of the box. He was even more frightened when the carton rattled and shook. Later he realized he must have travelled in a car, but at the time he knew nothing of cars.

The box was carried into a house, and when it was opened the frightened little puppy saw to his surprise he was under a tree covered with coloured

lights. Strange smells and noises were all around. He jumped out of the box and when hands tried to capture him he ran into a corner. There he sat, trembling with fright, under a chair.

He didn't notice at first, but a boy was sitting on the chair. A hand came down and very gently stroked the puppy's head. In return the puppy licked the boy's hand.

"Look, he's gone straight to Philip," someone said.

In a few moments the puppy was on Philip's lap. The boy was quiet, sitting somehow apart from everyone else in the crowded room. The puppy licked him again, and snuggled up to sleep in his arms. While all the others rushed around opening parcels, chattering and drinking, the quiet boy and the puppy stayed together.

The two other children in the family, Elizabeth and John, were both slightly jealous that the puppy made friends with Philip so quickly. They wanted to hold him as well, and to carry him around. Elizabeth was only

four, and when she did have a chance to pick him up, she squeezed his ribs so hard he ran quickly back to Philip again.

The puppy's only real memory of his first Christmas Day was making friends with Philip. He forgot how when he was first put out in the garden he hated the feel of the wet grass under his paws, and how he raced back into the house again. He forgot that when he was first placed in a basket with a bright new red blanket that he jumped out again, as he didn't realize this was his bed. Nor did he remember the little pieces of turkey for his dinner, although at the time he thought it delicious.

After the turkey he felt much braver and ventured into the middle of the room where he found a parcel that had not been opened. It was soft, and so he shook it, growling fiercely, as if it were a rat. Everyone laughed at him and he ran once more to Philip for safety and comfort.

That night, when he was left in the kitchen in his new basket with the red blanket, he whimpered and cried, for he was lonely. He did not understand he was the best Christmas present that the children had ever been given. All he knew was that he wanted to go back to the farm and curl up in the straw with his brothers and sisters and his mother.

After a while Philip's father came

down into the kitchen. He gave the sad puppy a hug, placed an alarm clock in the basket, covering it with a corner of the red blanket. He then put the puppy gently back in the basket and gave him a dog biscuit.

"Now you must sleep, little puppy," he said. "The clock may not be warm like your mother, but the ticking might stop you from feeling so lonely."

The puppy ate the biscuit slowly, crunching each bit carefully with his needle-sharp teeth, and settled down. The clock ticking was indeed a friendly sound. And so, at last, dreaming of Christmas trees and parcels, and especially of his new friend Philip, the little puppy slept.

Chapter Two

Give A Dog A Name

During the next few days the family all argued about what to call the new puppy. He was mostly white, with brown patches on his back and one big black patch over his left eye. This made him look both rather comic and a little fierce.

"Why don't we call him Sinbad, or Captain Flint?" the father suggested.

"I think we should call him Tiny," Elizabeth said.

"Don't be silly," said John. "He might grow into an enormous dog. I think we should call him Nelson. He had a patch over one eye."

"We could try Patch," the mother tried.

Everyone shook their heads.

"Or Wag?" said the father. "He's always wagging his tail."

The puppy wagged his tail at all these suggestions, for he could see they were talking about him. He really wanted Philip to be the one to choose his name. But Philip never joined in these discussions. In fact, Philip never talked at all.

In the end, Elizabeth came up with the right name.

"Let's call him Buttons," she said. "He's always trying to eat our buttons."

It was true. Whenever they lifted him up he chewed their buttons if he could.

The name seemed to suit him, and very quickly he learnt to look up whenever he heard, "Buttons! Buttons!"

He learned lots of other things in those first few weeks, too. He jumped into his basket whenever someone said,

"Basket!" in a firm voice. He was quickly house-trained, and enjoyed going out into the garden whatever the weather. It was full of exciting smells, and he used to bark at the cats next door. He liked digging holes in the flowerbeds and the lawn, but this made the family cross.

"Stop that, you bad, bad dog," they shouted, and Buttons would creep into his basket until they had forgiven him.

Nor was he popular on the occasions when he took a shoe or slipper to his basket to chew. The leather tasted marvellous, just as good as any bone. It made his mouth feel good, too, where new teeth were coming through. But he was always spanked when he chewed shoes. Then he would run to Philip. Philip was always kind to him.

But why didn't Philip talk, like the others talked?

Chapter Three

The Boy Who Didn't Talk

Buttons noticed other things about Philip. For instance, Philip did not seem to know when Buttons barked or scratched at a door if Philip couldn't see him. Also, Buttons discovered he could wake up Philip each morning by bounding onto the bed, but not by whining or barking on the floor.

Buttons was an intelligent little dog, and before long he worked out for himself that Philip couldn't hear.

Buttons was right. Philip had been born deaf, profoundly deaf in fact, which meant he could hear almost nothing at all. This makes learning to speak very difficult.

In every other way Philip was a normal boy. He could run and climb trees, and throw sticks and balls. He got hungry and tired like other boys. But like many deaf people, he was lonely. He found it hard to join in games when John and Elizabeth had other children around, and until Buttons came he used to spend a lot of time by himself. Now he was happy as he and the puppy understood each other. Neither of them could talk, but each had his own way of communicating, and they could be seen playing for hours.

What Buttons didn't realize at first was that Philip's mother was also deaf. She had learnt to talk, and with the use of a hearing-aid she could hear quite a lot. She could understand what other people said, too, by lip-reading: following the action of their lips as they were talking. She knew of the problems that Philip faced and helped him as much as she could.

Philip's teachers helped him too. He went to a special school for deaf children. A minibus came to collect him every day during term time. Buttons used to stand at the window with his tail between his legs and watch the minibus drive away. He was always waiting for Philip when he

returned. He would leap into the boy's arms and lick his chin. Then they would spend the rest of the day happily together.

Chapter Four

A Hedgehog

One warm spring day in March, Buttons found a hedgehog at the bottom of the garden. He sniffed at it and the hedgehog curled into a ball. Ouch! He hurt his nose on the prickles. He then ran round and round it in circles, barking wildly.

John and Elizabeth came out to see what was going on. When they saw the hedgehog still curled up in a tight little ball they were afraid that Buttons would hurt it or that the hedgehog would hurt Buttons. They tried to call Buttons away, but he took no notice of them.

John ran for help. His parents came,

followed by Philip.

"Here, boy! Here Buttons!" said the father sternly. Buttons carried on barking, as if he hadn't heard. Philip then tugged at his collar, but still Buttons wouldn't leave the hedgehog alone.

Then Buttons heard a new noise. He knew at once that Philip had made it. He stopped, looked round. Philip made the noise again. It was no more than a grunt from the back of his throat. Buttons knew, though, that this was important, and he went to Philip and licked him.

Philip's parents noticed and they made a great fuss of both Philip and Buttons.

"Philip talked!" Elizabeth said. "Philip talked!"

No one noticed the hedgehog slip away, but by the time they all stopped looking at Philip and Buttons it had gone.

A few days later Philip's teacher came to the house. Buttons could tell they were talking about him. Now

Philip's father took Buttons to the other end of the room and held him firmly by the collar while the teacher tried to make Philip call him.

Philip waved his hand as he always did when he wanted Buttons to come. But Buttons couldn't go as the father held on firmly to his collar. Again and again Philip waved his hand, but Buttons was always held back. Both boy and dog were puzzled.

Then they went down the garden to where Buttons had found the hedgehog. Once more they tried to make Philip call Buttons. Suddenly,

Philip knew what they wanted. He made the same noise he had made before. Immediately, Buttons' collar was released, and he ran to Philip and licked him. They repeated this several times.

That evening everyone in the family was happy, for Philip had started to talk.

"It's all because of Buttons," said Elizabeth.

Chapter Five

A Sad Picnic

Buttons was not more than nine months old when the family took him on holiday. They rented a house near the sea, and every day they all went to a beach.

It wasn't much fun for Buttons. The sea was salty, which he didn't like, and the sand got everywhere and made his skin tickle. Once they forgot to take fresh water for him to drink and he was expected to drink orange squash when he was thirsty. He didn't like that at all. Their sandwiches too, if he got a chance to eat one, were always gritty and tasted of sand.

If Philip hadn't been there Buttons would have hated every minute of it. As it was, Philip enjoyed digging in the sand, and exploring the rocks at low tide, and swimming, so Buttons stayed close to him and made the best of it. More and more now Philip talked to Buttons, developing a language which both boy and dog seemed to understand.

It had taken them a whole day to drive to the house near the sea. On the way they had stopped for a picnic on a common. The children had played in the tall green bracken, and Buttons had raced around with them. When the holiday was over, to Buttons' delight they stopped at the same picnic place on their return journey.

Once more the children ran along the little paths, through the green ferns, playing hide and seek. Buttons, as always, stayed close to Philip. Then, to Buttons' pure joy, a rabbit ran off in front of him. In a flash he was after it. What bliss! Buttons had never chased rabbits before, and now he forgot

everything with the excitement of it all. Chasing rabbits was the most wonderful thing he had ever done!

Later, much later, Buttons vaguely remembered hearing the family calling him, but he took no notice. He was just about to catch a rabbit at the time, and now, white tail and all, it disappeared down a hole in the ground. In a frenzy he tried to follow it, but the hole was too small.

"Just you wait, little rabbit! Just you wait!" thought Buttons, as he started to dig.

Earth flew, paws scrabbled and the hole grew bigger and bigger. Buttons dug on. Now he found he could get right down the hole. It was a tight squeeze, but he wriggled on and on down the dark tunnel. The smell of rabbits was everywhere, and thrilling beyond belief. All thoughts of Philip and his family had gone. He only thought RABBIT.

At last Buttons began to get hungry. He tried to get out of the hole. Going backwards was not so easy, as it dragged his hair the wrong way. Suddenly, he found he couldn't move forwards or backwards. His collar was caught on a tree root deep under the ground. He was stuck down the hole. No one could hear him bark, and he was a long way from home.

Back at the picnic place the family searched and searched for him, calling and whistling. Even Philip called him, in his own way. They still had a long way to go, so at last the father drove to

the nearest town and reported Buttons' loss at the police station.

"He's wearing a collar with a metal tag giving our address," he told the police.

"If he turns up, we'll contact you. Don't you worry."

The policeman was kind and tried to make them all feel better. But it was a sad, sad family that drove home that evening. In the back of the car Philip wept for he had lost the best friend he had ever known.

Chapter Six

Lost Dog

Poor Buttons! How he struggled underneath the earth to get free, but the more he pulled, the more his collar seemed to get caught. His paws became sore from scrabbling, and his eyes hurt from all the mud that got in them.

Eventually, he fell into a fitful sleep. Hunger woke him, and he tried again to get free. Throughout the night and the next morning Buttons struggled, rested, and struggled, rested, and struggled again in the dark.

Then, when he was weak from hunger, thirst and exhaustion, there was a "snap". His collar had broken. Buttons backed up the rabbit hole and into the fresh air. For some time he lay there, panting, too tired to move. He knew, though, what he had to do. When he felt a little stronger he went straight to the picnic place where he had last seen his family. It was deserted. There was no car, no family, no Philip.

"They'll come back for me," he thought, and he sat down to wait. He did not realize how long he had been down the rabbit hole and that by now Philip and his family were far away.

After a long wait, when no one had come, Buttons set off in search of food and home. At first he kept to the road. But cars were travelling along it very fast, and one nearly hit him. Now he was really frightened. He jumped into a ditch, and after a while set off across some fields. He didn't know he was going further and further from the town where his loss had been reported at the police station.

He passed several gardens, but none of them was his. They didn't smell right. On and on went Buttons. He drank from some rather dirty puddles,

and in one garden he found some food that had been put out for a cat. He wolfed it down, but apart from that he found nothing to eat. He sniffed round some dustbins, but the people in the house shouted at him to go away. He crept up the the next house, too desperate to care if they were friendly or not, and lay down in the drive.

A woman called out, "George, come and look here. There's a dog by the back door." She stroked Buttons and he tried to lick her hand, "Poor thing. I'll get you some milk," she said kindly.

"I think we should ask Charlie if the Animal Welfare Centre will take him in. Charlie's worked there for years, he'll know what to do," her husband suggested, "But there's no harm in giving the dog something to eat first. He's in a bad way, poor little thing. He's not much more than a puppy either."

Buttons found himself shut in a shed. It reminded him of the farm where he'd been born. He was given a bowl of food and then he slept on an old blanket in the corner.

He was woken by kind hands stroking him, and he heard a new voice say, "I'll take him to the Animal Welfare Centre and see if anyone claims him. He's a nice looking mongrel, and it's my guess he's only been living rough for a few days. Come on old fellow," Charlie added kindly to Buttons, and he lifted him into a basket, which he then carried to his van.

Chapter Seven

New Friends

Buttons was taken to a huge building and placed in a cage. There were dogs in other cages all around him. The noise of barking and whining came from every direction, but Buttons was too tired for it to disturb his sleep.

After a few days at the Animal Welfare Centre, with regular food and frequent runs in the excercise yard, he was feeling more like his old self. When a visitor walked down between the cages with the Animal Welfare Officer, Buttons pricked up his ears and wagged his tail eagerly.

"A nice bright mongrel here," the newcomer said.

The cage door was opened, and they

took Buttons apart from the other dogs and gave him various orders. Buttons, always anxious to please and quick to learn, sat when they told him. He ran to them when they called, and he turned his head quickly when they whistled or called from several directions.

"He's got good hearing and is extremely alert," the visitor said. "Do you know where he came from?"

"He was brought in by Charlie, one

of the people who works here. He was found by Charlie's neighbours, half-starved and with no collar."

"I'll take him then," the visitor said. "He's just the dog we are looking for," and he put Buttons in his blue van.

Buttons trusted this tall gentleman who seemed to understand dogs. As he sat in the van with him, he thought, "I do hope he is taking me home. How can I tell him Philip needs me?"

His new friend, who was called Tony, drove for about an hour, and finally they turned into a yard where there were several buildings. Buttons was taken inside one that looked rather like a stable and put into a pen. There was a big bed for him, and a bowl of water. There were two other dogs, also in their own shoulder-high pens.

"We're going to teach you all sorts of things," said Tony kindly, "but we won't start lessons until tomorrow."

Buttons wagged his tail. He felt sure they were going to be kind to him here, and he wanted to please Tony if he could.

That evening he got to know his two companions. Like him they were both mongrels, and had been found by Tony at rescue centres after being abandoned.

Duke, the largest, who had a lot of Alsatian in him, had been deliberately left far from home. He had been loved as a small puppy, but his owners had stopped caring about him when he grew too big. They thought he ate too much and he knocked things over in the tiny flat where they lived. One day they left him far from home, and he was found and handed in to the police who took him to a home for lost dogs.

Beauty was half-Labrador and half-spaniel. She was black with curly hair and floopy ears, and rather long legs. Her owner, an old lady, had died, and she had lived for only a few months with a family who had now gone to live in Australia. They had taken her to an animal shelter and asked them to find a good home for her. Then Tony came along and selected her.

Duke and Beauty had only been there for a few days and they were not entirely sure why Tony wanted them. Like Buttons they had to wait to find out.

Chapter Eight

Training

Buttons life changed completely now. The first thing that happened was that he was given a new name. Tony came in the next morning and said to him, "Right. From now on your name is 'Jogger'." He repeated the name, "Jogger", "Jogger" several times. Whenever Buttons pricked up his ears or came to him, after he said this name, he was given a tasty little biscuit.

"You'll soon get used to it," Tony encouraged. "All the dogs here are given new names as we never know what they were called before."

Buttons quickly learned to answer to

"Jogger", but he didn't really like it.

"I'll always think of myself as 'Buttons'," he thought. "I wonder why Tony chose the name 'Jogger' for me?"

Almost as though he could read his thoughts, Tony said one day, "Don't blame me if you don't like your name. I didn't choose it."

"More and more mysterious," thought Buttons.

Once Buttons had got used to his new name, he was shown a squeaky ball that Tony always carried. Each time Tony made it squeak Buttons had to go to him. Again, he was rewarded with a tasty little biscuit whenever he did so. After a few days it became second nature to go straight to Tony as soon as he heard the squeak.

Buttons was also given obedience lessons. Some things, like sitting when he was told, he had been taught before. Now he had to sit both when he heard the command, and when Tony gave a special hand signal. In the same way he was expected to lie down to a spoken order and at a hand signal. He had to "come" whenever Tony clapped his hands, as well as when he pressed the squeaky ball.

When he was on a lead he was taught always to walk on Tony's left side, and not to pull. If he went down to the village he was expected to stop at the kerb and wait quietly until it was safe to cross the road.

Duke and Beauty were being trained in the same way. All three were taught to pick up anything that Tony dropped, like a glove or a paper, and bring it to him. They were all encouraged not to bark.

This was especially hard for Buttons who had always enjoyed the sound of his own voice.

Chapter Nine

Alarms and Bells

After some weeks Buttons was taken into a bungalow that was in the yard where he lived. To his surprise no one lived there, although part of it was furnished like a home, with a lounge, dining-room, kitchen and bedroom. His training now took place in these rooms, and he was taught new skills.

When an alarm clock rang Buttons was expected to put his front legs on the bed in the bedroom, or jump onto the bed and wake up whoever was sleeping there. When he was used to doing this he was taught to come in from another room, whenever he heard the alarm, first pushing open the bedroom door, before waking up the person in the bed.

He was taught, if the door bell rang, to go and fetch Tony and take him to the door. It was the same with the telephone. When it rang he had to take Tony to it. Also, if the kitchen timer on the cooker went off Buttons had to take Tony to the cooker.

None of this was so very different from what he had done with Philip and his mother. He had always woken up Philip by bounding onto his bed, and he remembered going to Philip's mother and trying to tell her if someone was at the door. Most of the time she didn't know he was barking, so he had learnt to tell her by tail-wagging and pawing at her leg.

"You're quick all right, Jogger," said Tony, one day. "It's almost as if you had worked with deaf people before."

Now Buttons understood, partly, at least, what was going on. He pricked his ears and wagged his tail as he looked at Tony with pleasure.

Throughout the autum their training continued. It was the same for all three. Then Duke was taught to respond to a baby's crying. Whenever he heard the noise he had to fetch Tony and take him to the baby's cot in the bedroom. Neither Buttons nor Beauty were taught this. "Perhaps

Duke is going to a home with a baby and we are not," thought Buttons, using his intelligence once again.

There was one further lesson all three dogs were taught. Sometimes a fire alarm went off, if there was a lot of smoke in the house. It gave a high-pitched continual ringing sound, and the dogs learned that this was different from all the other bells they had been trained to respond to. Whenever they heard the fire alarm they were expected to wake up the person in the bed, but not to take him anywhere. They had to continue to lie on the floor to show that this was something different. This meant danger.

There were often visitors at the training centre. Some Americans came one day, and Tony demonstrated to them what Buttons could do. Buttons enjoyed showing off a little, and doing it all extra well. An American lady said, "My, I don't believe we have ever had such a quick little dog to train in the States." Buttons you may be sure, wagged his tail with pride.

One day a group of children came to see Buttons. He understood from what they said that their school had all saved up money to pay for his training. They had been asked to name him, and because most of the money they raised had come from a sponsored jog they had chosen the name Jogger.

"That explains it," thought Buttons, "but I still wish they'd chosen a nicer name."

Chapter Ten

Happy Christmas

Christmas was getting close, and all three dogs were ready to go to their new homes. Beauty and Duke left first. Each was given a special orange collar and lead, which is the symbol used by dogs which have completed their training with Hearing Dogs for the Deaf. Also they were given certificates, to show they could go on public transport, like dogs for the blind.

Gillian, who worked with Tony at the centre for Hearing Dogs for the Deaf, took them to their new homes. While Tony was responsible for training the dogs, her job was to make all the arrangements with the families where the dogs were going, and to work with the deaf owners for about a week, explaining what each dog could do, and make sure the dog responded to the new owner. Buttons overheard her telling Tony how well both Duke and Beauty had settled down, and how useful they were.

He also heard her say that his new family wanted him to arrive as close to Christmas Day as possible. He hoped this meant he was going to a home with children.

At last, on Christmas Eve, he was given his new orange collar and lead, and was driven away by Gillian. For two hours Buttons sat in the car and thought how sad it was that he always lost his best friends; first Philip, and now Tony.

Then the car drew up outside a house, a house Buttons knew well. There, on the doorstep, waiting were Philip, John, and Elizabeth.

Gillian was rather surprised to see a well-trained dog jump straight into a strange boy's arms. Philip and Buttons were so delighted to see each other again they didn't notice the fuss going on all around them. "It's Buttons. It's

Buttons. I know it's Buttons," Elizabeth kept saying.

Meanwhile Gillian was talking to Philip's mother. "It's quite extraordinary. We trained the dog for you, not for your son, although of course we knew he was deaf too."

"Quite," said Philip's father. "It was only when we had Buttons that we

realized how much a dog can help a deaf person. Buttons was marvellous with Philip, but at the same time he was a real companion to my wife during the day, and helped her in all sorts of ways, although he wasn't trained. After we lost Buttons we thought we would never find another dog that was so intelligent, so we applied to Hearing Dogs for the Deaf for a trained dog."

At last peace was restored. Buttons stopped licking everyone, and they all stopped hugging Buttons. Gillian showed them how Buttons had been trained, and said she would come back straight after Christmas and work with them for about a week until Buttons was fully settled again, and using his training.

The next day was like Buttons' first Christmas, but better. The Christmas tree was there again, with its coloured lights, and the parcels underneath. The turkey for Christmas dinner was as delicious as before. Buttons' basket was in the kitchen, with a new blanket

in it, for the family had thought they were getting a new dog. When he went to sleep that night Buttons was deeply contented for the first time in months as he was home once more where he really belonged.

Upstairs, Philip thought, "There has never been a happier boy."

Chapter Eleven

A Famous Dog

Buttons' story does not end there.

He did everything he was trained to do extremely well, and was a tremendous help to Philip's mother, and to Philip when he wasn't at school. Philip was talking much more now, and had several friends at school.

Some days Buttons went to school with Philip to show other families what a dog trained by Hearing Dogs for the Deaf can do. Tony used to come to these demonstrations, and Buttons was always delighted to see him.

Then, one day, a film company rang up and talked to Philip's father for a long time. The director had heard about Buttons and wanted to make a film about him. At last Philip's father agreed.

For several weeks people came and went from Philip's home. There were lighting technicians and sound technicians, a camera crew, a director and a producer and their assistants, and many other people besides. The family got used to a crowded house, and behaved as naturally as possible while they were being filmed.

The film was shown on television, and Buttons became a celebrity overnight.

Now he was invited to go to dog shows, and demonstrate his skills. He was recognized everywhere. He was also asked to visit several schools where the pupils were interested in raising money to train more dogs. Philip and his mother went to all these places with Buttons, and they became celebrities too.

Buttons' face, with the famous black patch over one eye was used on packets

of dog biscuits, as an advertisement, and the money the firm paid was handed on to Hearing Dogs for the Deaf, to train even more dogs. A book was written about Buttons, and the story of how he got lost was told in full, as well as how he was picked out by Tony at the Animal Welfare Centre and trained.

Like all celebrities he had a full and busy life, but he was never happier than when he was at home with the family he loved so much.

You may not believe in miracles but

you can believe in luck. It was a lucky day for Philip when Buttons first came to his home, and it was a lucky day for Buttons when he came back home to Philip. If ever Buttons has to be given a third name perhaps it should be Lucky.

A special fund has been set up to sponsor a dog to be named Buttons. The money will be used to train the dog so that it can be given to a family like Philip's. Please send your donations, however small, to:

Hearing Dogs for the Deaf Training Centre
Buttons
2 Chinnor Hill
Chinnor
Oxon 0X9 4BA

If you live in Australia you can write for more information to:

John Bartlett
Vice Chairman
Hearing Dogs for the Deaf Inc.
G.P.O. 1687
Adelaide
S. Australia 5001

If you live in New Zealand you can write for more information to:

Hearing Association Inc.
P O Box 7099
Wellesley Street
Auckland
New Zealand

Other Hippo Books You Will Enjoy:

SHEPHERD'S PIE

Dorothy Clark

ISBN 0 590 70310 2 70p

"Jack the giant's mother was an excellent cook and she believed in using natural ingredients. So cottage pies had to have *real* cottages in them — with the result that for miles around there was not a cottage left standing."

The Woolly family were particularly worried. Their cottage had been taken by Jack's mother, and that was bad enough, but they could see there might be more trouble ahead. Mr Woolly was a shepherd. What if the giants decided to try shepherd's pie?

In the face of such danger, Sandy and Polly Wolly knew that they must take drastic action. What they did makes a most satisfying conclusion to this very funny story.

HARRIET AND THE CROCODILES

Martin Waddell

ISBN 0 590 703099 £1.00

Harriet spells trouble, for teachers and for everyone else, too. She is very upset when her pet yellow snail disappears but looks forward to selecting a new pet during the class trip to the zoo.

Why is it that only Harriet thinks her crocodile is sweet and charming?

An hilarious story introducing Harriet who is already a firm favourite with 7-9 year olds.

HARRIET AND THE HAUNTED SCHOOL

Martin Waddell

ISBN 0 590 70441 9 £1.25

Finding a horse for Anthea to practise sitting on wasn't much of a problem for Harriet. But choosing a place to keep it was! The Games Cupboard provided a cosy home and the horse could take it's excercise at night!

But the late-night ghostly hoofbeats terrified the cleaning lady, Ethel Bunch. There was only one solution: the Slow Street Vigilantes and the Anti-Harriet League had to join forces — and set up a phantom trap!

Harriet is back!